A Monster and a Child

Mistle Onoel

Ukiyoto Publishing

All global publishing rights are held by

Ukiyoto Publishing

Published in 2022

Content Copyright © Mistle Onoel

ISBN 9789364948357

All rights reserved.
No part of this publication may be reproduced, transmitted, or stored in a retrieval system, in any form by any means, electronic, mechanical, photocopying, recording or otherwise, without the prior permission of the publisher.

The moral rights of the author have been asserted.

This is a work of fiction. Names, characters, businesses, places, events, locales, and incidents are either the products of the author's imagination or used in a fictitious manner. Any resemblance to actual persons, living or dead, or actual events is purely coincidental.

This book is sold subject to the condition that it shall not by way of trade or otherwise, be lent, resold, hired out or otherwise circulated, without the publisher's prior consent, in any form of binding or cover other than that in which it is published.

To Kimmy, Chloe, Ben, and Elvin

Contents

It	1
Alter Game	7
Not Kimmy	11
Monstrous City	16
Monsters	20
The Portal	27
The Oracle	35
Memories	39
From Kimmy Walker	45
About the Author	*46*

It

Shhh!
Shhh.
Shhh…

We need to be very quiet. Any minute now, **it** will come out.

Do you know **it**? I bet you do! **It** lives under my bed. And I know **it** lives under your bed, too. How do I know that? Well, I just know.

During the witching hour, at 12 in the midnight, **it** slowly crawls out of my bed. Then **it** walks around my room. I don't know what **it**'s doing. I haven't checked, and I don't want to check.

I'm sure **it** is some hideous monster. **It** must be some black blob with green ghoulish eyes. Just thinking of **it** makes me shudder. So I really don't want to see **it**. That's why I stay under my blanket and pretend to be asleep.

Do you hear that? Listen carefully. There's a scratching sound underneath my bed. **It**'s trying to get out. Be very still. Don't move around. Or else **it** will find you. Thump. Thump. Thump.

Blobs don't have feet so they should just skid around. I have no idea why **it** makes so much noise when walking.

Ah! I got it! **It**'s a blob with two big feet. Just imagine that. **It**'s really hideous.

It's approaching me. Hold your breath. I know **it**'s checking if I'm still awake. But I won't move an inch. Then **it** won't know that I'm actually wide awake.

It's walking away now. **It**'s going through all my things. I really, really hate **it** because of this. Every night, I clean up my things. But in the morning, everything is all over the place. And mommy gets angry with me. Oh how I wish I'm brave enough to tell **it** to stop making a mess!

Hmmm? I smell something. It's good. It's making my tummy grumble. Wait. I know that smell. It's my donut! Is **it** going to eat my donut? Oh no! That can't happen.

"Yippee!" I heard **it** say in a raspy, ugly voice.

It's really my donut.

"Hey!" I shouted as I removed the blanket.

I saw **it**. **It**'s just as I thought **it** to be – black blob with green ghoulish eyes. And holy guacamole! **It** really has two big feet! What's more is that it has two hairy hands! So hideous!

It turned around with **its** mouth wide open, the donut in **its** hand about to enter. I saw **its** eyes slowly widen. Then my precious donut fell onto the ground.

"Aaaaaahhh!" **it** screamed.

"Aaaaaahhh!" I screamed back.

"Aaaaaahhh!"

"Aaaaaahhh!"

"Aaaaaahhh!"

"Aaaaaahhh!"

"Aaaaaahhh!"

We paused for a moment and panted. Then we went on.

"Aaaaaahhh!"

"Aaaaaahhh!"

"Aaaaaahhh!"

"Aaaaaahhh!"

"Stop!" I shouted. "I should be the one screaming. Why are you screaming?"

"No!" **It** shouted with its ugly voice. "I should be the one screaming. Why are you screaming?"

"I'm a human and you're a monster. It's only right that I scream."

"That's right! You're a human and I'm a monster. That's why I screamed."

"Why? What's wrong with being a human?"

"Well, what's wrong with being a monster?"

I frowned. "Stop copying me!"

"You copied me first! I screamed then you screamed."

We glared at each other. I really, really, really hate **it**.

I got off my bed and walked towards **it**. **It** wasn't really scary now that I was closer to **it**. **It** wasn't really big that **it** towered over me.

"Well, you're in my room. So go back to your place." I pointed under my bed.

It hmmph-ed. "I can't go back until the witching hour is over."

"Then just stay under the bed."

"I don't want to! It's dirty. And dusty. And dark. And so tight. I don't like that place!"

"That's where you belong. You're so ugly and hideous and… ugly and hideous."

"Hey, that's mean! You made me this way!"
"It's not mean. It's true. I am a very honest girl. I am not very bad. And I don't make monsters."
Grumble.
It picked up the donut while glaring at me. I sat at the edge of my bed without breaking eye contact. I didn't want to lose!
I looked at the donut that I made being gobbled by **it**. That donut, I made it for my teacher. My teacher said that I was bad. But you know, I was not very bad. I was bad sometimes. But I was good sometimes, too. But my teacher never saw me being good. So I made a plan to make her see my good side. I made that donut to give it to her during class. But seeing the donut now, it's so hideous. It's burnt to crisp. It's better for the hideous donut to enter **its** hideous mouth.
"Ah." **It** burped.
It smelled so bad I had to cover my nose.
"Just to let you know, I didn't say you're bad. Or you're mean. I just said your words are mean."
"It's the same thing."
"No, it's not. Are you stupid?"
"I'm not stupid!" I rose up from my bed.
I was really not stupid. I could do math pretty well, you know. Do you want me to show you? Well, let's have 13 and 12. Well… Hey! You should try to answer it yourself. I know it but I won't tell you.
"Your words are mean. But you didn't take away the donut from me. It's yours, right?"
I nodded grudgingly.

"Then you gave me food. That's not mean. That's nice. So I'm stupid if I call you mean. And you're stupid because you say you're mean."

I glared. "Just go back home."

"I said I can't go back until the witching hour is over. Look. It's still 23 minutes past 12."

"So you'll be staying here for many hours?" I asked with my brows furrowed deeper.

"3 hours and 37 minutes to be exact."

"Why? Just go back. What will you be doing then? Make a mess again?"

"What make a mess? I don't make a mess. It's art. Okay? You're so impolite. You don't know art at all."

I remembered all the mess **it** made after visiting my room every day. It's not art at all. **It** scattered my books all around my room. Some pages even got torn! I got some spanking from mommy because of that. **It** also threw my stuffed toys onto the floor. And **it** did many more.

Just because **it** thinks it's art doesn't mean it is. It's totally trash.

"Just don't do it. Art or whatever you call it," I said.

"But then what do I do? I don't want to be idle. That's boooòooring. And you know what happens when you're bored? You do crazy things. Do you want me to get bored?"

"Fine. Just do whatever you want except that art thingy."

I climbed onto my bed. This monster was not scary at all. It's worse than that. **It** was annoying. Really, really annoying. It would've been better if this monster were scary.

Alter Game

Okay. I'd had enough. This monster was reaaaaaaaally annoying. The lower half of my body was covered with my blanket. My hands were on my tummy. My eyes were shut. I was ready to sleep. But **it** kept on roaming around me.

This monster reminded of Marianne. You think this monster's annoying? Wait 'til you meet Marianne. She's my classmate. We're always classmates. And I hated that. She's this Miss goody-two-shoes while I was the bad girl. Bad girl was an understatement. They said I was a monster.

One time, she bumped into me in the hallway. My lunch was all over the floor. I got angry. But I didn't say anything. I just picked up my food and walked away. The following day, I heard about me making Marianne cry. Apparently, somebody saw her running after me to apologize. But I just ignored her.

"She's so mean," my classmates whispered.

My teacher made me apologize to her in front of the class. It was embarrassing.

I hated good girls. But I hated my teacher even more.

I opened my eyes. **It**'s standing at the right side of my bed. **It** was giving me a sheepish smile. I rose up.

"What?!"

"I want to play a game."

"Then play. Stop bothering me."

"But I want to play with you. You said I can do whatever I want. And I want to play a game with you. It's either we play a game together or I do art."
"Wow. Are you threatening me?"
It shrugged.
"I have school in a few hours. I need to rest," I said.
"I know you sleep after I'm gone. Don't even try to lie."
It's true. I really only slept after **it**'s gone. But could you blame me? How could I sleep with my heart beating so loud? It's too noisy. I wasn't relaxed enough to go to dreamland. Imagine having a monster coming out under your bed every night. You wouldn't be able to sleep either.
"Let's get this over with."
"Yippee!" **It** jumped. "Come here and sit on the floor."
"What are we playing?"
"My favorite, the alter game. It's very easy. You just got to imagine yourself becoming someone else or even something else! Then you wait for a few seconds and you become exactly that. Fun, isn't it?"
"I can't do that. I'm not a monster. Hello?"
"No," **it** said. "You can do it. You're even doing it now."
I raised one of my brows. "And how in the world am I doing it?"
"Look at me. I look like this because this is how you think of me. Didn't you learn that at school? What does your school even teach you?"
"My school teaches us that there are no monsters."

"Your school is stupid." **It** leaned forward. "Then let me just do what your school failed to do. It's like this. Every child in the world has a monster under the bed. And every monster looks according to what the owner of the bed believes. Your mind is weird." **It** looked at its body. "Anyway, you have that power."
It sounded pretty cool now. I was getting a little bit excited. I knew something nobody else knew. I was pretty sure Marianne didn't even know about this. I was one step ahead her now. Hahahaha! I'm so smart!
"So I just imagine it, right?" I asked.
"Yes. But before that, I need to share my heart with you first."
"Is that really necessary?"
"Very necessary. You have a human heart. Only monsters can alter appearance. So if you have even a bit of my heart, the game will recognize you."
"I'm following. But how are we going to do that? I hope we won't be doing anything weird like drinking your blood."
"Drinking my blood?" **It** laughed. "That's nasty! We just need to hug."
I broke into a smile. **Its** laugh was weird but in a funny way. The ha's are not connected. It sounds like a toro grunting ha.
"A hug?"
"Yep. A hug." **It** squinted **its** eyes at me.
"What?"
"Don't tell me you don't know why we need to hug."
I was starting to warm up to **it** but then **it** decided to annoy me once again. **It**'s really like Marianne. You

know, Marianne was a big know-it-all. She's a smartass. A braggart. A wiseacre. A smarty-pants. Do you know about the moon man story? I know you've heard that there's a man in the moon. And it's true. There really is a man there. But it's a different type of man. It eats other people! A cannibal! And where does he get his food? From our world. He is into tweens, kids aged 8-12. He peers through his telescope to find a kid who is still awake at night. He uses the moon's gravity to take any child he likes. I'm 9 so I make sure to close my windows at night. I told my classmates about this during break time. It was the first time they stayed so close to me! They didn't run away like before. Then Marianne chimed, "That can't be real." I told her that it's real and I swore on my life. But she went on talking about how the earth's gravity is much stronger than the moon's and how gravity can't just choose one object to pull. Blah blah blah.

"We need to hug," **it** continued, "because it's one way for us to share our full trust. We are showing are backs to each other without any protection. And the only person or monster or whatever that we trust to that extent is ourselves. Got it?"

I nodded. **It** beckoned me for a hug. Eeek! So slimy! And hairy! Twenty seconds in and we're still hugging. "Aren't we supposed to stop now?" I asked. **It** shook **its** head. I just let my body go limp. I had no idea it would take about half an hour.

When we let go of each other, I immediately dusted my clothes. Nothing stuck on me but it still felt icky. I just had to do it.

Not Kimmy

I'm Kimmy Walker. I'm Kimmy Walker. I'm Kimmy Walker. I'm Kimmy Walker. I'm Kimmy Walker. I repeated my name in my head many times with my eyes closed. I was in a yoga sitting position. It said that I needed to make sure that I believed that I was really me. How stupid was that? Of course I believed I was me. When had I ever been not me? I'd always been me.

I had been doing it for minutes. I got excited about this game because it sounded cool at first. I didn't know it would be this tiring just to play it. Was this even playing?

It told me to wait when it signaled for me to change the spiel. There were 5 spiels. First is: I'm Kimmy Walker. Second is: I'm not Kimmy Walker. Third is: You're not Kimmy Walker. Fourth is: You're whatever or whoever I want to transform into. Last is: I'm whatever or whoever I want to transform into.

Was this actually a lie? Was it just pranking me? I peeked through my left eye. It was doing the same thing as me. It was mouthing something, too. I tried to read its lips. It was something like Rulley. I guess it's real. I focused again.

I felt myself slowly drifting away. Away and away and away. It shrieked in a different voice. I opened my eyes. I shrieked as well. It looked like me. No. It was me.

"You wanted to be me? That's disgusting!" We said at the same time. We rose to our feet and looked at the mirror.

"We switched," I said. "There must be something wrong. Are you sure you gave the right instructions?"

"I'm pretty sure I gave the right instructions."

"Then what's happening?"

"I think you just want to be me," **it** said.

"Me wanting to become you? No way! I've never ever thought of becoming a monster. Maybe it's you who just wants to be me. But that's okay. I totally understand. I'm amazing. A lot of people are jelly of me."

It scratched its head. "Ah! I know. We transform according to what we want, right?" I nodded. "But there's another way for us to transform, too."

"What way?" I asked.

I looked okay with my yellow top and black striped pajamas. My hair was tied in a bun and it had gotten messy because of all the scurrying I did while waiting for **it** to come. My bangs were still in place though.

"We can also transform according to what we believe we are. And this is much, much stronger because it is the feeling of belief, not just want," **it** explained.

"There must be some mistake. I don't want to be a monster. And I certainly don't believe that I'm a monster. Other people believe that, but I don't."

"What was that?" **It** asked. "Never mind. It's not important. What you think is not important. The game decides and the game does not lie. It never lies. So there is definitely no mistake here."

"There is." I insisted. "I really told the game who I wanted to be."

"Didn't I just explain that part to you?" **It** rolled **its** eyes. "Well, we can't change this. No matter how many times we play it, it will still be the same."

"Let's just try again. We never know."

We did it again. We sat on the floor in the same position as before. We did all the necessary rituals. Then we officially started the game. This time, I was sure that it would go right.

I'm Kimmy Walker. I'm Kimmy Walker. I'm Kimmy Walker. I'm Kimmy Walker. I'm Kimmy Walker. I'm not Kimmy Walker. I'm not Kimmy Walker. I'm not Kimmy Walker. You're not Kimmy Walker. You're not Kimmy Walker. You're not Kimmy Walker. You're not Kimmy Walker. You're Marianne Allen. You're Marianne Allen. You're Marianne Allen. You're Marianne Allen. I'm Marianne Allen. I'm Marianne Allen. I'm Marianne Allen. I'm Marianne Allen.

I focused on the game. I shooed away any thoughts that tried to distract me. So I was really confident when I opened my eyes.

"See? No changes."

I frowned. "Again."

But it was still the same. So we did it again. And again. And again.

"This is tiring. Let's stop. It will always be the same. Let's just accept this. The game has decided that you are my alter and I am your alter," it said.

"No. Let's try again."

"No. We've done it many times already. Doing it once more won't change anything."
"Let's just try one last time."
It squinted its ghoulish eyes. "Okay. One. Last. Time."
We positioned ourselves. I had gotten the hang of it. You could say that I was an expert at the alter game already. I did it quite fast this time. So I opened my eyes.
My eyes widened. I looked to my left and then to my right. It didn't take long for a frown to form on my face. We were in a totally different place! And so many monsters were around us!
"Rulley," I whispered. Rulley still had its eyes closed. "Rulley," I tried again. I had to make my voice soft to avoid attracting attention from those monsters.
I bit my lip. And my frown grew worse when I met eye-to-eye with a 3-eyed monster. It was coming towards me. I hit Rulley many times without breaking eye contact. I was afraid of breaking it. In movies, people who took their eyes off the monster always died. And I really mean ALWAYS.
"RULLEY!" Well, that did the job?
It opened **its** eyes. "What? I was concentrating."
"Look behind you."
It was standing right behind Rulley. I knew it had business with us. It stopped right there.
Rulley turned **its** head. "Oh, it's you, Purthree."
The so-called Purthree shifted its eyes onto Rulley. "Do I know you?" it asked with a gruff voice.
"It's me, Rulley."

Purthree paused for a moment. "Alter game?" Rulley nodded. "That's good. You finally got to play it. I sent your performance assessment already. You can check it out."

"Thanks."

Purthree then continued on its way. When it was beyond hearing distance, I grabbed Rulley by the collar. But I did it gently. It still had my body.

"Where are we?" I asked.

Rulley swatted my hands away. "We're just in Monstrous City. Stop being dramatic."

"Monstrous what?"

"Monstrous City." It rolled its eyes. "My home."

Monstrous City

I always thought that Rulley's home was under my bed. I never thought it's actually just a door to the world of monsters. It's very strange, you know. I thought that all monsters looked the same, like Rulley. But they came in different shapes and sizes. Some didn't even look like monsters at all. There's a red fluffy ball bouncing all around. There's also a worm-like yellowish monster. It's disgusting rather than scary. Blurghh. Then there's a badly made monster. It's like a child's drawing. To be fair, most monsters looked like children's drawing.

But hold your horses. Don't even think that this is some cute place. There were also monsters that were reaaaally scary-looking. You might even piss your pants when you see them. One had its body twisted all around. Its hair was very messy and its dress was soiled. Its eyes were wide open and it wore an unfaltering grin! The horror! I looked away the moment I saw it.

Let's stop talking about monsters. I don't want to think of it ever again. Yes, EVER. Here in Monstrous City, monsters lived in places called Hollows. It looked just like a one-story house on the outside. Very small. When you go in, you'll directly be in the elevator. I was really shocked when I saw the buttons. There were hundreds and hundreds of them. They were on the walls, on the ceiling, and some were even on the outer sides of the floor.

"You pressed F789. You will arrive shortly," a robotic voice announced.

"F789?!" I looked at Rulley.

"You're really dramatic. It's just F789."

I rolled my eyes. "Does that mean the 700th floor?"

"F is the sixth letter of the alphabet. Every letter has 1000 floors. And you've been insisting that you're smart since a while ago so you MUST know it already."

I crossed my arms and said, "Of course."

Rulley's really taking me for a fool. So annoying. I was in its body now so I could just easily pounce on it. But how could I do it when I saw my beautiful face?

"It's 5739," Rulley said.

"What?! 5739?! How big is this Hollows thing?"

"Very big. We have 136 batches of the alphabets actually. Thankfully, I'm in the first batch so it doesn't really take a long time."

"Shocks!"

The elevator dinged. The doors opened and the moment I stepped out, I was inside a bedroom. It's a little bit smaller than mine but it's still quite spacious. It had a single bed. Beside it were a desk and a chair. On the wall, there was a certificate. It said: Monster Academy. Certificate of Completion. Monster Trainee X003. Average: 93%. That reminded me of something.

"Oh no! I have a math test today," I said. "I need to go back home. Rulley, take me home this instant. I can't be absent. Just being there gives me 10 points already."

"We can't just go home whenever we want. That's not how things work. We need to wait for the portal to open."

"When does it open?"

"During the witching hour."

"No! I can't wait for that time. That means I'll be absent the whole day," I explained.

I shouldn't have played this alter game in the first place. If only I knew. But I didn't. And I couldn't turn back my time.

"You don't have to worry about that," Rulley said. "The time in your world and the time here are very different. They're not dependent on each other. So you never know when the portal opens. Somebody just announces it."

"I don't care about that time thingy. Just tell me. I will be able to attend my classes, right?"

Rulley nodded. I sighed as I plopped onto the bed. It felt bouncy. I lied down. It's really comfortable. If you have a chance to visit here, you should try the bed. It'll make me you fall asleep in no time. When I opened my eyes, it was dark already.

I rose up. "Rulley, aren't we going to eat anything? It's dinner time." I stopped. Rulley was eating already. It was slurping some noodles. "Hey, why didn't you wake me up?" I walked towards it and took the only seat left. "You're in my body," it said. "Monsters don't feel hungry."

I frowned. "Who said that? That's totally wrong. You have a stomach, right? Then you should feel hungry."

"You think that I don't feel hungry."

"I don't think that way at all. I think I feel hungry now," I said.
"But I've never felt hungry when I was in my original body. That only means one thing. You think I don't feel hungry," it explained.
"Why do you keep on talking about what I think? They're not connected."
Rulley looked at me dead in the eye. My face looked so serious. I never knew I could make that face. Had I known that, I would've worn it every time somebody messed with me at school. But thinking about it again, it wouldn't be so good. They would just call me monster. People really didn't know what a monster was. They hadn't seen Rulley.
Rulley sighed. "You really don't know much about anything."

Monsters

"Let me tell you from the very beginning," Rulley said. "Do you see that statue over there?" Rulley pointed out the window and I moved my head a bit to see it. I could see it but I couldn't understand what it was. Was it supposed to be a monster? "That's Milstoy, the very first monster." I frowned. "I don't see a monster. It's confusing. Like math."
"Then you can say that math thing is a monster. Anyway, Milstoy came into Monstrous City when everything was nothing. Literally nothing. Only Milstoy was here. Then Milstoy heard a mother's voice and it said: 'If you don't sleep, the monster will come out and eat you.' And Milstoy, who was formless that time, started to have a form. It was slow though. It began with the general shape of the body. Then the more intricate details."
"I don't see any intricate details at all."
"Please don't interrupt me."
I pursed my lips and leaned back. Then I nodded once to let Rulley continue.
"The statue there is Milstoy's final form. Then Milstoy saw a light that seemed to suck everything. And Milstoy was everything here during that time. That thing is actually the portal to your world."
I gasped.

"Why are you gasping?" Rulley asked. "It's not that shocking."
"Just continue," I said.
A lot of my classmates gasped when the teachers said something not even close to being shocking. But they liked it maybe because it was somewhat a proof that the students were listening to them. So I just wanted to practice. I promised myself that I would do it as well once I got back home.
"Milstoy went to your world. And when he came back, more monsters came. You know, our place is called Monstrous City because Milstoy's child is really smart beyond her years and she shouted monstrous city when she saw Milstoy."
"Do you mean monstrosity?"
"Yeah. Monstrous City. And didn't I tell you don't interrupt me?" Rulley crossed its arms.
"Oopsie," I said with a hint of sarcasm. Then I gave Rulley a sheepish smile.
"Now where was I? Let's go back to the more monsters that came into being when Milstoy came back. I think you've noticed that the monsters look different. It's like we have different creators. Well, that's because we really have different creators. My creator is you. Whoever is the monster's child is the creator of that monster. I started out as a story that your dad used to tell you when you were younger. Actually, most monsters that you saw started out that way. The moment you doubted that I might be real, I began to exist. Then I slowly took the form that I have now based on what you believe. I appear under your bed

because that's what you believe. You believe that I don't feel hungry so that body doesn't feel hungry at all. Because you believed that I am this way, I became this way."

Does this mean I'm like a god? Oh my golly! I could turn Rulley's body into something else, something that I needed. Maybe I could Rulley into me and make it my double. Then I would just believe that it was very smart, very kind. The perfect daughter, the perfect student, the perfect classmate, the perfect girl, the perfect Kimmy! Then everybody would love me. They would stop avoiding me because of my dad. I would be too perfect that they couldn't resist me even though I was my dad's daughter, even though I looked like my dad.

Even my foster mommy would finally let me call her mommy in public. I wouldn't have to call her Mrs. Johnson at all. Then she would wake me up with a kiss on my forehead. When I go to the dining room, I would see my favorite spaghetti ready for me. And mommy would also drive me to school like the other kids. I hope the car would break down so that we could walk hand in hand. That would be great!

At school, teacher Rosie would flash a smile at me and call my name sweetly. If she sees me hesitating to answer, she would encourage me. When I don't understand the lesson, I could go to her office and she would tutor me. She wouldn't be scared of me because of my resemblance to my dad.

During break time, my classmates would always invite me to play with them. Then I wouldn't have to tell them made-up stories so they would stay with me. I would even crack jokes and they would laugh. And when my jokes become too lame, they would make fun of it and we would laugh again. Marianne could even be my best friend!

Then on my 10th birthday, they would surprise me. We would have lunch together then we would take a picture.

"I never thought I would say this about my body, but your smile is giving me the creeps," Rulley said. "Why are you being like this?"

I grinned. "Rulley, you're the best. Why didn't you ever tell me this?"

"Because you never asked?"

"Oh, yeah. That's right. I should've asked you." I looked out the window. "Since you got here because I believed in you, will you also be gone once I stop believing in you?" Rulley nodded. "Well, aren't you lucky? You're going to be here forever," I said.

"You will die one day."

"But that's still a long time. You will be experiencing lots of great things because I will never forget you."

How could I ever forget something like this? It was the best thing that ever happened in my life.

"No. You will forget me."

"I won't."

"And how do you know that?"

"I just feel it. This is one of the most extraordinary things that happened to me. How could I forget it, Rulley?"

"Humans always forget. When they find something better, they forget."
"Oh my golly!" I exclaimed. "It's that monster again."
Rulley looked out the window. "Haja?"
"If you're talking about that one with a twisted body, messy hair, and a soiled dress then yep, I'm talking about that."
"That's Haja."
"I've seen it twice in one day. My eyes have been damaged. I need to wash them."
"Hey, that's not nice."
"Sorry. I was just kidding. I wouldn't really wash your eyes, you know. It would be painful for me since I'm using your body now," I explained.
"I'm not talking about that. I'm talking about disrespecting Haja. It's not Haja's fault. Haja was created that way. And I honestly don't see anything wrong. A monster is still a monster."
"I'm thinking Haja is a monster-er. But yep, it's not Haja's fault. But this means that its creator is very imaginative. Look at how scary Haja is. I can't bear to look at it."
"That's a given. Haja's child has been believing in Haja for 37 years. Maybe tomorrow Haja will look scarier to you because its child keeps getting more creative every day."
"37?" I asked. "Isn't that too old?"
"37. As what I can remember, he started believing in Haja when he was 11 years old."
"Oh my golly! That means he's now 48, right? He's a child no more. He's an adult."

I couldn't believe it. That man was a grownup already yet he was still scared of monsters. I always believed that once I grew up, I would be fearless. That's what I saw. Now I was starting to think of my future. What if I would be like that guy? What if I become soooo creative that I would turn Rulley into something really scary? That couldn't happen! And it wouldn't. I'd make sure it woudln't. I could control my monster. Surely, I could control it tomorrow the way I could control it now.

Rulley said, "He's still Haja's child. And what's so wrong about an adult feeling scared?"

"It's scary," I said. "Everybody will call me a scaredy-cat."

"But is it not only true?"

"It is true. But then nobody will help me. They will just tell me to grow up because I'm a child no more."

You think I was wrong because your mommy and daddy or your mommy and mommy or your daddy and daddy or just your mommy or just your daddy take care of you when you're scared, right? Well, that's because you're still a child. Once you're a teen, they will start telling you to be brave. They won't stay beside you when you're scared.

Even now, nobody stays by my side when I'm scared. How much more when I grow up? It's scary to be a grownup.

"Don't worry. I won't tell you that at all," Rulley said.

"Why? Because I'm special?" I grinned and did the grace face.

Rulley grimaced. "Stop doing that to my precious face. You're not special," it said. "I'm a monster. You're supposed to be scared of monsters. It's normal."
Ding!
"It's open!" Rulley rose up from its seat. And we scurried down.

The Portal

I could hear my footsteps as I ran as fast I could. I couldn't wait to go home. After the math test, I would do what I planned just before. Rulley would be the perfect Kimmy. And then I would take its place later on.

But it took us too long to leave. Every time the elevator stopped in Rulley's place, it was full. Like reaaaally full. There was no breathing space at all! Rulley told me that we could squeeze in. It said that it always did that.

I frowned at Rulley. That's totally impossible!

"Can't we go when we are the only monsters left?" I asked. "I don't feel comfortable being in close contact with them."

"I'm fine with that. But remember that there are 1000 floors for each letter in the alphabet. Can you wait that long?"

"If we wait that long, will the portal be closed by the time we get there?"

Rulley thought for a while then looked at me. "I'm not quite sure. I never waited."

I gathered all my brain cells. We couldn't risk it. It would be too tiring to wait for the next opening of the portal. Besides, I'm in Rulley's body. If it is used to it, then I won't have any problem at all. I just got to make sure that my body doesn't get squashed.

I hugged Rulley and once the elevator dinged, we squeezed ourselves in. I never let Rulley out of my grasp and that was the best decision I ever made. Hear this. There was a spiky monster on my left and a flaming one on my right. And that's not all. There were more monsters that were weirder. But I haven't the vocabulary to accurately describe them. Just think of the worst.

Thank goodness that Rulley's body is a blob. Well, it's thanks to me that its body is like this. So I guess it's only right that I feel grateful towards myself. Thank you, self.

Ding! We're finally out.

"My body is convenient, right?" Rulley said.

"Very convenient," I replied. "But Rulley, I have a question."

"Shoot."

"If I can decide your appearance, does that also mean I can decide your personality?"

"Why?"

"It's the only explanation that you're so cool."

Rulley laughed. "You don't really decide it but you're a part of it. You created me so I can only follow the blueprint of your heart. Doesn't it work that way in the human world also?"

I looked down. "Yeah, it does."

We walked in silence from then on. I looked around and I saw more monsters. By that time, I got the hang of it. You could even say I'm a monster expert. I know what kind of a person the child is based on the child's monster.

That monster must have a child that's scared of the ocean. That one's child must be scared of homework. That child is really cool. How was he or she able to make a homework monster? I never even thought of that.

"We're here," Rulley said.

I looked around. There were lots of monsters waiting there. And when I say lots, I really mean lots like lots and lots of monsters. But I could still see the portal. It was so big.

Near the portal, I could see another monster that was bigger than normal. It looked like a standing newt. It was looking at a list. Once it gave the go signal, the monster could enter the portal.

"Rulley, I think that monster's checking the list of monsters," I whispered.

"That's Porcius," Rulley replied. "Porcius is the one who makes sure that all the monsters go to their children. You know, some monsters sleep in."

"Really?"

"Yeah. That's why Porcius is here to make sure that doesn't happen."

We moved up in the line. "Then that means he knows all the monsters, right?"

"Yep."

"That's a big problem for us, Rulley. Porcius will know that I'm not a monster."

Rulley thought for a moment. "Yeah. But it's not really a big problem. Not even a problem actually."

"And how do you know that?"

"It's weird that a human is here, but we're not doing anything bad. We're not breaking any rules. Porcius can't say you're bad just because you're weird."

"Still, that means only of us one can go back," I said. "And it's most probably me because I'm in your body."

"Hey! Move up!" a monster chimed in.

We hurriedly moved up. We made sure to move up every now and then. It wouldn't be good news if that monster would flare up because we were too caught up in our conversation.

"I think so, too. But isn't that great because it's you who needs to go back? But I also don't think so because I'm the monster so I need to be there," Rulley explained.

I still don't get how Rulley didn't see any problem. If I was the only one who got back, it would be disastrous! I was in Rulley's body. Yes, the Alter Game. But we had to hug. Who was I going to hug? My mommy? No. My big sis? No. There's nobody to hug.

"We're next," Rulley whispered.

The monster before us entered the portal, and my heart was beating fast. Porcius scanned the two of us and fixed his glasses.

"So you have a name now," Porcius said. "Rulley."

I forced a laugh. "Ha. Ha. Ha. Nice to meet you, Porcius. I'm Rulley."

Porcius looked at me. "I was not talking to you, child." It then shifted its gaze at Rulley. "You may enter."

"Porcius, can she go with me?" Rulley asked. "She's actually my child and we just got here because we played the Alter Game. When the portal for coming

back here opened, she was sucked in as well because she was in my body."
Porcius tsk-ed. "Try it out then."
Rulley nodded. I gave Porcius a sheepish smile then walked towards the portal. I breathed deeply. Just to be safe, I reached my hand out first. But it never got through. I pushed harder and harder.
"We have the answer. The portal recognizes monsters," Porcius said.
"But I'm a monster. In my world, I'm a very bad monster. Don't you know Leo Walker? He did something bad. He killed somebody. A baby. And I'm his daughter, Kimmy Walker. I have his blood. I should be able to go through."
Porcius fixed its glasses. "You think you're a monster, but you're not. And the portal confirms that. The portal is never wrong."
"As you said, she's not a monster. So she doesn't belong here. She needs to go back to her world," Rulley explained.
I nodded in agreement.
"The only way for you to go back is through this portal. You need to be a monster to go through this portal. Instead of explaining to how much you need to go back home, why not start working on becoming a monster?" Porcius said.
"That's right," the monster behind us seconded and pushed us away.
We went out of the line and the monsters' sendoff went smoothly again.
"What do we do now?" I asked.

Rulley was quiet while pursing its lips. It looked at me and grinned. "Let's go."

I totally had no idea where we were going. But I just followed it. We were heading to the apartment so I thought its plan was to play the Alter Game. We stopped in front of the apartment and then turned to our left. Rulley sighed and started walking. I walked faster to be at the same pace as Rulley.

"Where are we going?" I asked.

"The Oracle."

"Oracle? Is it something like a magical monster?"

"Yes and no."

I stopped Rulley.

"What?" Rulley asked.

"I have an idea. Why don't we just play the Alter Game?"

"It doesn't work here. Let's go." It continued walking.

I grabbed its hand. "Have you tried it?"

"No, and there's no need to. It doesn't work."

"Let's just try please," I begged.

Rulley squinted its eyes at me. "You're acting too different. Do you see something here?"

I looked down and nodded. There's a dark forest right in front of us. I started seeing it the moment we took a left turn from the apartment.

"That's good then. It's working," Rulley said.

"What's working?"

Apparently, the Oracle was a magical place that allowed monsters to prove they were really monsters. They had to start from the apartment and start walking to have the Oracle. They had to do it again and again until they got it. That explained why Monstrous City was empty save for the portal and the apartment. That also explained why a lot of monsters were walking weirdly and why a lot of them were not inside the apartment. The only way for them to have a room in the apartment was to be approved by the Oracle.

Rulley explained that whoever got the Oracle would start seeing something else. Most of the time, monsters had to defeat whatever was there.

"I can't go in there," I said.

"It's okay. It's not hard. When I had the Oracle, I just had to eat a little child."

"Eat a little child?" I gasped. "Rulley, you're a monster."

"I am a monster," Rulley said. "But it's not real. What happens in the Oracle is this: the child has a standard of what a monster is. The monster has to achieve that standard. And for you, a monster is somebody who eats children. I think I ate the 4-year-old or 5-year-old you."

"But I don't have a child because as what Porcius said, I'm not a monster. So why am I having the Oracle right now?"

"It's me. I'm your child."

I frowned. Could you blame me? My brain was not used to complicated things. Monstrous City really liked to make things complicated. My life was simple. For example, my dad was a bad person so I'm a bad person. But in here, I'm a good person.

"When I was in that body," Rulley pointed at me, "You were my child. Now you're in my body so I am your

child. But my idea of a monster is still based on your idea. I already told you that your heart is the blueprint of my whole self."
"This is really not good, Rulley. I know what monster is there and I don't want to be that monster."
"It's okay, Kimmy. You are not really going to become a monster. Besides, don't you wanna go home?"
I looked at the forest and thought for a moment.
"Well?"
"Okay," I said softly.
"That's more like it! Let's go."
Rulley skipped while he walked. I guessed he also wanted me to go home. That's good. But if you saw us, would you laugh at me for being a scaredy-cat? Rulley's there walking in a relaxed manner while every step I took was hesitant. But I saw the dark forest. Rulley didn't. So don't ever call me a scaredy-cat.
I walked faster and grabbed Rulley by the hand. It looked at me and I sent a worried smile. Rulley got my message right away and held my hand tight. We entered the forest.

The Oracle

I remembered this place. It was the forest right behind our old house, when daddy and I were still together. Before I knew what was happening in this place, I just thought daddy loved to eat ketchup.

Daddy always went home at 11pm. His clothes always had red stains on them. He explained that he just had his dinner. "Ketchup," he said. I was 5 so I believed that he just loved ketchup. I loved ketchup, too. So I knew where he was coming from.

But one time, daddy went home too late, like really late. And I got scared being left alone. The week before that, I heard something moving under my bed. "It's the blob monster," I thought. So instead of staying there, I went out to look for daddy.

I saw Ms. Johnson who was having a road trip on her own. I waved my two hands and she walked to me. "Can you go with me to the forest?" I asked. Ms. Johnson said yes without asking. I knew why she did that. She loved my daddy and she wanted to be my mommy. She often told me how great it would be if her daughter and I would become sisters. I was excited at the idea.

But when we went there, we saw daddy killing somebody. Daddy ate children for dinner. I froze in the spot while Ms. Johnson shouted, "Monster!" Her screams caught daddy's attention. He looked at us. Daddy had green, ghoulish eyes.

The police eventually arrested my daddy, and everybody in the village pushed me to Ms. Johnson. I was quite happy. At least I would be with somebody who loved me but I was wrong. Mommy didn't want to be my mommy.

We went to the next village to start anew but it was just impossible. Even more so with the fact that my teacher there knew what happened. How would she not know? It was her son.

My teacher didn't tell anybody about it but she treated me differently. She never believed in me. She never supported me. She never let me try. So whenever I saw how she treated Marianne, I felt a little bit angry.

I stopped walking. Rulley stopped, too. "Take a breath," it said. And I did. One more step and a turn then I would see it.

"Let's go," I quietly said.

We took a step and turned to the left.

"What do you see?" I asked.

I pursed my lips. "It's the same thing."

My teacher's son was there all tied up. He was struggling just like what happened on that day. When he saw me, he started thrashing around.

"Rulley, he's scared of me. I'm really a monster."

"Please don't kill me!" he begged.

I looked at Rulley and shook my head. "I can't do it."

"Just try one more time," Rulley suggested.

I looked at the boy again. Was I really going to become like my daddy like they said? Or was I already like my daddy?

I fell on my knees and cried. "I'm sorry." I crawled to Rulley and begged, "I can't do it. I don't want to be like my daddy. Please. Just let me stay here. Everybody says that I will turn out to be just like daddy. But I don't want that. And I'm not really bad. I may have failed the math test many times. I may have forgotten to do my homework a lot. I may have told lies every day. But I'm not a bad. I'm not a monster. I don't want to be a monster."

Rulley pulled me into a hug while I kept apologizing. He caressed me back as he whispered, "I'm sorry."

I stopped crying only because I was too tired. I fell asleep. When I woke up, I was back in Rulley's apartment.

"Would you like some milk?" Rulley asked with a cup in its hand. I nodded. "I got this milk from Haja. Haja's child loves to drink milk and the milk is something premium. This will make you feel better." It handed the cup to me.

"Thank you," I said. I took a sip. "I'm sorry, Rulley."

"Why are you apologizing? You did nothing wrong."

"But the Oracle... Maybe we won't see it again and maybe you're tired of taking care of me already."

"I should be the one apologizing. I told you to try when you already showed that it was too much for you," Rulley said. "Many say that trying is the greatest talent of human beings. But maybe not all humans are talented. And maybe that's okay. I should've listened to you the first time. I'm sorry."

"Thank you, Rulley, for letting me give up." Rulley smiled and sat beside me. "I guess this is my new home now," I said.

"Kimmy, I really love having you here. You're a great child, but you don't belong in this place. The portal and the Oral proved that."

I looked down. "Do I need to have the Oracle again?"

"Oh, no, no. I won't let you go through that again. There's another way."

"The Alter Game?" My ears perked up.

Rulley chuckled. "How many times do I have to tell you it doesn't work here?" It chuckled again. "There's a monster called Elem. Elem eats memories."

Memories

"What about it?" I asked. I had a feeling where this was going. But I didn't like it. So maybe if I acted dumb, Rulley wouldn't go there.
"This place exists only because you believe in us."
"So you want me to stop believing in you and everything here? But I can't do that. With everything that I've been through, it's hard to erase."
"That's why we need Elem. Elem will eat your memories. If you don't have any memory of this place, then you will stop believing. You will automatically go back to your world I think."
I knew it. But it wasn't what I wanted. Sure, I wanted to go home. But I didn't want to go home that way. I would forget the only place that wouldn't let me out just because I wasn't a monster. It was the only place where I wasn't a monster. If I forgot about this, I'd go back to that time when I always waited for mommy to tell me I wasn't a monster. I'd go back to those days when I copied Marianne to be treated like a child by my teacher then be dejected because no matter what, she wouldn't say those words to me.
"Rulley, can I just stay?"
"Huh? But what about your math exam? You were fussing over it just a few moments ago," Rulley said.

"Yeah," I said quietly. "But I don't want to forget that I'm not a monster."
"Why would you forget? You don't forget who you are. You shouldn't forget that."
"But I forgot that for many years."
"Is it because of what other people said? I heard your mom shout at you once." I nodded. "That's sad," Rulley continued, "to forget who you are. Then why don't you just tell people who you are?"
"It doesn't work that way. We can lie easily. We don't have your portal and the Oracle."
"Well, how about not telling people who you are? Just focus on telling yourself who you are. Isn't that what matters most?"
It was a great suggestion, but I already thought of it before. "I tried that for many years, too. But I lost to what other people said. Adults are just very strong, you know. If I were an adult, I would tell good things about every kid I meet."
Rulley sighed. We were quiet for a moment. I was about to tell Rulley to not mind about to lighted up the mood. But it excitedly said, "I have an idea! Why don't you write about everything that happened here? When Elem eats your memories and your back, you can read it and then remember everything."
"That's good!" I agreed. "Do you have paper and pen?"
Rulley went away for a moment and came back with the things I just asked for. "Aren't these mine?" I asked. It smiled sheepishly. "Why do you have them? I didn't take you for a thief, Rulley," I joked.

"Hey, I didn't steal them. One time you almost caught me and started throwing things in your defense. These accidentally stuck to me."
"Oh, sorry. Wrong number." I went to the table and Rulley followed suit. "But where should I start?"
It thought for a while then said, "What about the part where we tried to get through the portal?"
"But if I read this, I'll find it weird. How did you I even get here in the first place?"
"Good point," it remarked. "What do you think about the witching hour when I just got into your room?"
I gave Rulley a thumbs up, and I started writing. Looking back at it, it's very funny. We were shouting at each other for quite a while, then we argued as to who was acting appropriately. But I think I was right. Rulley was a monster.
"You really like to prolong your words," Rulley commented.
"I want to feel how I felt when I read this. And I want to feel a bit relaxed when I start out. You know, I stop reading when I feel like the author will be writing something serious. So it's got to be childish at first to make me start reading." I looked at it. "By the way, are you a girl or a boy?"
"Is that important?"
"I need to know that so that I can write the proper pronouns."
"You mean the he and the she?"
"Yup! Wow, you know it. Do you have a school here?"
"I heard you cramming in the middle of the night. But I remember that there is it, too." Rulley really heard a

lot of things. I wonder what else it heard. Hopefully it's nothing embarrassing.

"That's for something else. Just tell me. Are you a girl or a boy?"

"You tell me. You control me."

"Shall I make you a boy? Or a girl?"

"Hey, can't you just let me be?"

"Hmmm, okay. It'll sound weird but I think the pronoun it is the best for you since it respects who you are. You're okay with it, right?"

Rulley nodded. I continued writing. The story's mood began to grow gloomy as I neared that Oracle part. Rulley noticed me hesitating and read what I was writing. It suggested to take a short break, but I refused. I had to finish it at that moment or else I would forget.

I said, "Rulley, you said some nice words here. You sure you're not some wise man?"

"Call me the Wise It."

"You're really sticking to that, huh?" I chuckled.

"Of course," Rulley said. "I'm proud of who I am."

I squinted my eyes. "Are you bragging that you know who you are?"

"You can brag, too. You know who you are already, right? Or did you just want me to say?"

I nodded and laughed. When I was almost finished, I asked Rulley if we would wait for Elem to be back. But it said that Elem was already back. The portal had opened for the coming home of the monsters. I finished the story while Rulley went to get Elem.

I stretched out and helped myself to some milk. I didn't know writing was very hard. It's like forcing myself to go to a world and then writing everything before it vanishes. I wonder how it is for other writers. They need to write a world that doesn't actually exist. I'm lucky mine is real. Otherwise, I'd be in big trouble.

"Are you done?" Rulley asked.

I took one last sip from my cup and said, "Yup." I saw a monster behind Rulley. It was Elem. Elem was just a crystal ball with feet and hands. "Nice to meet you, Elem." I looked at Rulley. "Rulley, can I continue writing until the last moment?"

"But you said you're done," Rulley said.

"What about this part? I can't leave it out."

"Alright. You can write until the last moment."

"Oh and Rulley, where will I find this notebook?" I asked.

Rulley explained, "It will go back with you so long as you hold it. It will be in its original place, in the place where it should've fallen had I not been there when you were throwing things."

"Got it."

"Can we start now?" I nodded. "Elem's not much of a talker so I'll do the talking. Come here and stand right before Elem. Since you want to continue writing, Elem will just put its hands on your shoulders."

I did so. Then Elem started saying something I couldn't understand. I didn't know where the voice was coming from because I didn't see its mouth. We stayed like that for a few minutes, then I started to forget how I got into Monstrous City. It was happening. After that,

I couldn't remember the Oracle, but I remembered Rulley and I talking about it.

I turned to my right and looked at Rulley in the eyes. "Bye," I mouthed.

And the last thing I saw was Rulley in my body saying, "Goodbye."

From Kimmy Walker

Hello, Kimmy. This is Kimmy Walker. But it's been 17 years. I'm 26 already.

It's good to know that you found who you are. Even if it's not real, at least you know that you're not a monster but a child. I'm sorry you had to make that Monstrous City just to hear what you'd always wanted to hear.

If you can read this Kimmy, I want to tell you that yes, you're indeed a child. I'm sorry it took this long for an adult to tell you this. You don't have to try so hard to be the perfect child. Even if you're not perfect, you're still a child.

And Kimmy, I would like to apologize for one more thing. I'm sorry that I really became a monster. Do you hear that sound? It's the police coming for me. They took a long time to find my location and that's why I got to read your story. But don't worry because you're not me. You're not the monster; I am. You're just an 11-year-old girl. You're just a child.

You see, I just found this notebook today while trying to hide. And I felt compelled to stop for a few hours to read this. How could I not stop? I just realized that there was a time in my life when I was really a child. But I grew up forgetting this and nobody ever told me that I was just a child. So let me be the one person, the one adult to tell you this: you are not a monster.

You are not a monster. You are a child.

About the Author

Mistle Onoel has been teaching for two years. She has heard countless stories from her students and wishes to tell the world, especially adults, about them. For she, too, has her own experience of being wrong just because she is a child.

www.ingramcontent.com/pod-product-compliance
Lightning Source LLC
LaVergne TN
LVHW041637070526
838199LV00052B/3420